This book belongs to

Princess _Smolen_

# The Royal Disney Princess Club

Every Disney Princess Treasures Her Friends

Friendship

Story adaptation, crafts, and activities by Kris Hirschmann
Photography by White Light Incorporated, Bethel, CT
Design by Mark A. Neston Design

© 2008 Disney Enterprises, Inc. All rights reserved.

Published by Scholastic Inc., 90 Old Sherman Turnpike, Danbury, CT 06816.

For information regarding permission, write to: Disney Licensed Publishing, 114 Fifth Ave., New York, NY 10011.

ISBN-13: 978-0-545-04835-4    ISBN-10: 0-545-04835-4
U.K. ISBN-13: 978-0-545-08548-9    U.K. ISBN-10: 0-545-08548-9

Printed in Singapore

First printing, June 2008

# Disney PRINCESS

# Snow White
## and the Seven Dwarfs

A Storybook with Crafts & Activities

SCHOLASTIC INC.

New York   Toronto   London   Auckland   Sydney
Mexico City   New Delhi   Hong Kong   Buenos Aires

Once upon a time there lived a vain and wicked queen. Each day, she addressed her enchanted mirror: "Magic Mirror on the wall, who is the fairest one of all?" And each day, the mirror replied that the Queen was the most beautiful.

But one morning, the mirror told the Queen that it was Snow White, her stepdaughter, who was the fairest in the land.

The Queen was enraged! She had given Snow White only rags to wear and treated her as a servant. Surely the mirror was wrong!

Outside at the courtyard's wishing well, Snow White was happily singing while she worked.

Just then a handsome prince rode past and heard her singing. He looked over the wall and instantly fell in love with the beautiful girl. As he serenaded her with his own song, Snow White found herself beginning to fall in love with him, too.

Watching the way the Prince sang to Snow White, the Queen became so jealous that she decided to get rid of her stepdaughter forever. The Queen called a huntsman to her throne. "Take her far into the forest," she commanded, "and kill her."

The Huntsman led Snow White deep into the forest, but he couldn't bring himself to harm her. Instead, he told Snow White of the Queen's wicked plot. "Quick, child. Run away!" he urged.

Terrified, Snow White fled into the forest to hide from her stepmother.

As night began to fall, Snow White became hopelessly lost. Tired and afraid, she fell to the forest floor and began to cry.

When the animals of the forest spied the poor girl, they took pity on her and led her through the woods to a tiny cottage. "Oh, it's adorable!" exclaimed Snow White.

The Princess knocked at the door, but when nobody answered, she decided to go inside.

"Oh, my!" she exclaimed. The cottage was a mess! She counted seven tiny chairs around the table and wondered who might live there. "Must be seven little children," she guessed.

Snow White decided to clean the house from top to bottom. "Then maybe they'll let me stay," she said hopefully.

With help from her animal friends, Snow White swept the floors, washed the dishes, and cleaned the windows. The little cottage was soon gleaming.

After all her hard work, Snow White found herself feeling very sleepy. She made her way upstairs; and with a yawn, she lay across a row of tiny beds and fell fast asleep.

Snow White had no idea the cottage belonged to Seven Dwarfs named Doc, Grumpy, Happy, Sleepy, Sneezy, Bashful, and Dopey. While the Princess slept, the Dwarfs were heading home after a hard day's work in the diamond mine.

They were very surprised to find a stranger asleep in their cottage!
"It's a girl!" declared Doc.

"She's beautiful," said Bashful.

Just then Snow White awoke. "Why, you're little men!" she said,
surprised. "How do you do? I'm Snow White."

At first, the Dwarfs weren't sure what to think. But they quickly
grew to love the kind princess.

Meanwhile, the Queen once again asked the Magic Mirror
who was the fairest one of all. "In the cottage of the Seven Dwarfs,"
the Mirror replied, "dwells Snow White, fairest one of all."

The Queen was furious! "I'll go myself to the Dwarfs' cottage," she declared. First she created a magic potion, which transformed her into an old peddler woman. Then she mixed another potion to make a poisonous apple. Whoever bit the apple would fall into a deep sleep, and only Love's First Kiss could break the terrible spell.

The next morning, after
the Seven Dwarfs had left for
the mine, the disguised queen
appeared at the cottage window
with an apple. "Like to try one?"
she asked slyly, offering the
poisoned fruit to Snow White.

"They do look good," thought Snow White. She took a bite
of the apple and a moment later fell to the floor in a deep sleep.

"Ha, ha, ha!" the evil queen cackled, as she ran out of the cottage. She would once again be the fairest of all!

Meanwhile, Snow White's animal friends had found the Dwarfs and told them the Princess was in danger.

The Dwarfs rushed home just in time to see the old woman running away. "After her!" they cried.

The Dwarfs chased the woman up a steep, rocky mountainside. Just when it looked like she might escape, a bolt of lightning struck, causing the wicked queen to lose her footing and fall off a cliff—gone forever.

When the Dwarfs returned home
to find Snow White asleep, they
were filled with sorrow, thinking
she had died. They made a golden
bed for their beloved princess and
kept watch over her day and night.

Then one day, after searching far and wide, the Prince finally found Snow White. Recognizing her as the lovely girl he had fallen in love with at the wishing well, the Prince leaned over and gently kissed her lips.

And with that kiss, Love's First Kiss, the Prince broke the evil queen's spell. Snow White awoke from her deep sleep and smiled with delight when she saw her true love standing beside her.

The Prince carried Snow White to his horse. "Good-bye," she said fondly to her dear friends, giving each Dwarf a kiss on the forehead.

Then the Prince and Snow White left for his castle, where the two would live happily ever after.

# The End

Every Disney Princess Treasures Her Friends

friendship

# This month's princess theme is friendship.

These crafts and activities will show you different ways
to treasure your friends.

# Snow White's Crafts & Activities

The Seven Dwarfs would do anything in the world for their beautiful friend, Snow White. Turn the page to discover Snow White's crafts and activities all about friendship!

Snow White

Sne

# Best Friends Mirror

Every day, a magic mirror tells Snow White's stepmother who is the fairest of all. Make a magic mirror for yourself and one for your best friend. Every time she sees it, she'll remember how much you treasure her!

With a grown-up's help:

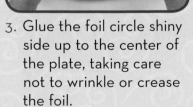

1. Tear off a sheet of aluminum foil that is just larger than the CD. Lay the foil on the paper towel and lay the CD on the foil.

2. Press down on the CD while you carefully run the toothpick lightly around the edge of the CD. Repeat 2 or 3 times until the toothpick has cut cleanly through the foil.

3. Glue the foil circle shiny side up to the center of the plate, taking care not to wrinkle or crease the foil.

Crafts & Activities

4. Use the marker to write, *Mirror, mirror on the wall, who is the best friend of all?* around the edge of the plate.

5. Tape the plastic spoon facedown to the back of your plate as shown. This is your mirror's handle.

6. Decorate the edges and the handle of your mirror with sequins, jewels, stickers, ribbon flowers, or anything else you like.

**♡ Royal Idea**
Give the finished mirror to your best friend. Each time she looks into her mirror, she'll see the words you wrote. Who is the best friend of all? *She is,* of course!

# Picture Perfect

With a grown-up's permission, get a camera. Stand in front of a mirror with your best friend and strike a pose. Point the camera at the mirror, then take the picture. (**Hint:** This works best when the camera's flash option is turned off.) It's a fun and funny way to take a best friend's self-portrait!

# Snow White and Friends

Snow White loves her friends, the Seven Dwarfs. Make a deck of cards featuring the Princess and her pals. Then use your cards to play the friendship games on pages 34–35.

Doc

Dopey

Snow White

## What You Need

- Copier
- Four 8½- x 11-inch (22- x 28-cm) sheets of paper
- Crayons, markers, or colored pencils
- Scissors
- Glue stick
- 16 blank 3- x 5-inch (7.5- x 13-cm) index cards

With a grown-up's help:

1. Make two copies of the left side of page 33 and two copies of the right side, enlarging it 200 percent.

   **Royal Idea**
   If you want, skip steps 1 and 2. Just look for pictures or stickers showing Snow White and the Seven Dwarfs. Make sure you find two images of each character, then glue or stick each one onto an index card.

2. Color the 16 characters with crayons, markers, or colored pencils.

3. Cut out the rectangles of Snow White and her friends. Glue one character to each index card. When you are done, you will have a deck of 16 cards—two cards for each character.

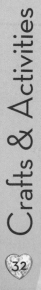

Crafts & Activities

Snow White

Dopey

Happy

Grumpy

Bashful

Doc

Sleepy

Sneezy

Crafts & Activities

33

# Always Remember Your Friends

In this game, Snow White and the Seven Dwarfs are all mixed up.
Use your memory to match up the characters and win the game!

### Number of players:
You need two players for this game.

### Get ready:
Mix up the 16 cards you made on pages 32–33. Lay them
facedown—four across and four down—on a table.

Bashful

Bashful

### How to play:

• One player turns over any two cards. If the characters
on the cards match, the player gets to keep the cards. If the
characters on the cards do not match, the player turns the cards
back over.

• Now it's the next player's turn. The second
player turns over any two cards. She keeps
the cards if she makes a match, and turns
them facedown if she does not.

• Players continue taking turns,
following the rules above, until
all of the cards have been
matched.

• Players count their matches.
The player with the most
matches wins the game.

# Fishing for Friends

In this simple go-fish game, Snow White and the Dwarfs are trying to find their matches. The first player to match up all her cards is the winner!

## Number of players:
You need four players for this game.

## Get ready:
- All four players sit in a circle.

- Mix up the 16 cards and lay them facedown in a pile. Players take turns picking four cards from the pile. If a player draws two matching cards, she returns one card to the pile and chooses a new one. Players are not allowed to look at each other's cards.

## How to play:
- The first player looks at her cards. She asks any other player for the matching card of her choice. Instead of asking out loud, however, she whispers her question into the player's ear. By doing this, she keeps everyone else from hearing what cards she is holding.

- If the chosen player has the card that was whispered, she must hand it over. The first player now has a matched pair. She places her matched pair facedown next to her.

- Every time a player makes a match, she gets another turn. When she fails to make a match, the turn passes to the next player.

- Players take turns asking for cards and making matched pairs until one player has no more cards. That player is the winner!

# Wishing-Well Bank

Snow White whispers her dreams into the courtyard well. One day, she asks for true love and her wish comes true! Make *your* wishes come true with this adorable wishing-well bank.

## What You Need

- Recycled plastic drink mix container with lid, 2.1 ounce (59 g)
- Scissors
- Paintbrush
- Paint (any color)
- Markers, stickers, string, and other items to decorate your well
- Pencil or pen
- 8½- x 11-inch (22- x 28-cm) sheet of paper (any color)
- Glue stick or white glue

With a grown-up's help:

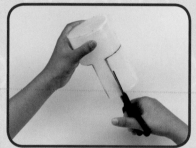

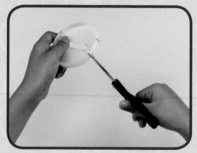

1. Take the lid off the drink mix container. Cut away the sides of the container as shown. When you are done, you will have a short round container with two long tabs sticking up.

2. Cut side slots along the edges of the lid as shown. The side slots should be just wide enough to go around the tabs from step 1. The center slot should be large enough for a coin.

3. Place the lid on the container as shown. Paint your bank and let it dry. Decorate your bank with markers, stickers, string, or anything else you like.

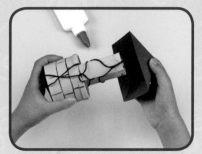

4. Copy or trace the shape and the lines below onto the colored paper. Cut out the shape along the solid lines, but not along the dashed lines.

5. Fold along the dashed lines. Overlap the side flaps so that the bottom edges line up. Then glue the flaps together to complete your roof.

6. Glue the roof to the container's long tabs to complete your wishing-well bank.

**Royal Idea**
Make wishes for your friends whenever you drop coins into your wishing well. Close your eyes as you make your wishes and believe that your dreams will come true!